W9-CCZ-621

I Am a Bird

Dana Walrath

Illustrated by Jaime Kim

atheneum
ATHENEUM BOOKS FOR YOUNG READERS
New York London Toronto Sydney New Delhi

atheneum

ATHENEUM BOOKS FOR YOUNG READERS
An imprint of Simon & Schuster Children's Publishing Division
1230 Avenue of the Americas, New York, New York 10020

For information about special discounts for bulk purchases, please contact Simon & Schuster Special Sales at 1-866-506-1949 or business@simonandschuster.com.
The Simon & Schuster Speakers Bureau can bring authors to your live event. For more information or to book an event, contact the Simon & Schuster Speakers Bureau at 1-866-248-3049 or visit our website at www.simonspeakers.com.
Book design by Debra Sfetsios-Conover
The text for this book was set in ITC Cerigo Std.
The illustrations for this book were rendered in watercolor and digitally.
Manufactured in China
0218 SCP
First Edition
10 9 8 7 6 5 4 3 2 1
Library of Congress Cataloging-in-Publication Data
Names: Walrath, Dana, author. | Kim, Jaime, illustrator.
Title: I am a bird / Dana Walrath ; illustrated by Jaime Kim.
Description: First edition. | New York : Atheneum Books for Young Readers, [2018] | Summary: A boy and his father enjoy a day at the beach and see how things are connected, as a bird that can fly leads to a fly that will land, that leads to land stretching to the sea.
Identifiers: LCCN 2017000718|
ISBN 9781481480024 (hardcover) | ISBN 9781481480031 (eBook)
Subjects: | CYAC: Ecology—Fiction. | Nature—Fiction. | Beaches—Fiction. | Fathers and sons—Fiction.
Classification: LCC PZ7.W16618 Iad 2018 | DDC [E]—dc23
LC record available at https://lccn.loc.gov/2017000718

To my sons Nishan, Tavid, and Aram
—D. W.

For my dad, Tae Wook Kim, who always encourages me
—J. K.

I am a bird. I fly.

I’m a fly. I land.

I am land. I stretch to the sea.

I'm the sea. I crest.

I'm a crest. I warn.
I'm a worn old shoe in the sand.

I am sand. I stick.

I'm *a* stick. I float.

I'm a float on a fisherman's line.

I'm a line. I tug.
I'm a tug. I tow.

My toes get tickled by kelp.

I am kelp. I branch.

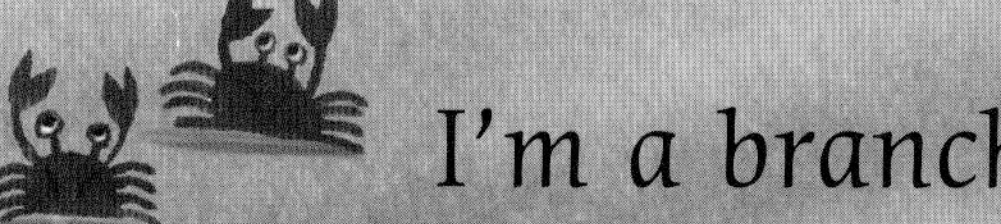

I'm a branch. I snap.

I'm the snap of a crab's sharp claw.

I'm a claw. I burrow.

I’m a burrow. I warm.
I warm my hands in my wings.

Flap fly.

Float high.

Snap, tickle, sway.

I am a bird. I glide
into arms open wide.

I’m the hands that hold

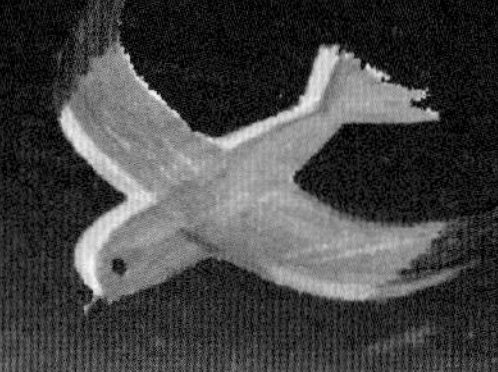

and the eyes that shine . . .

when it's you
and it's me

and the sea.

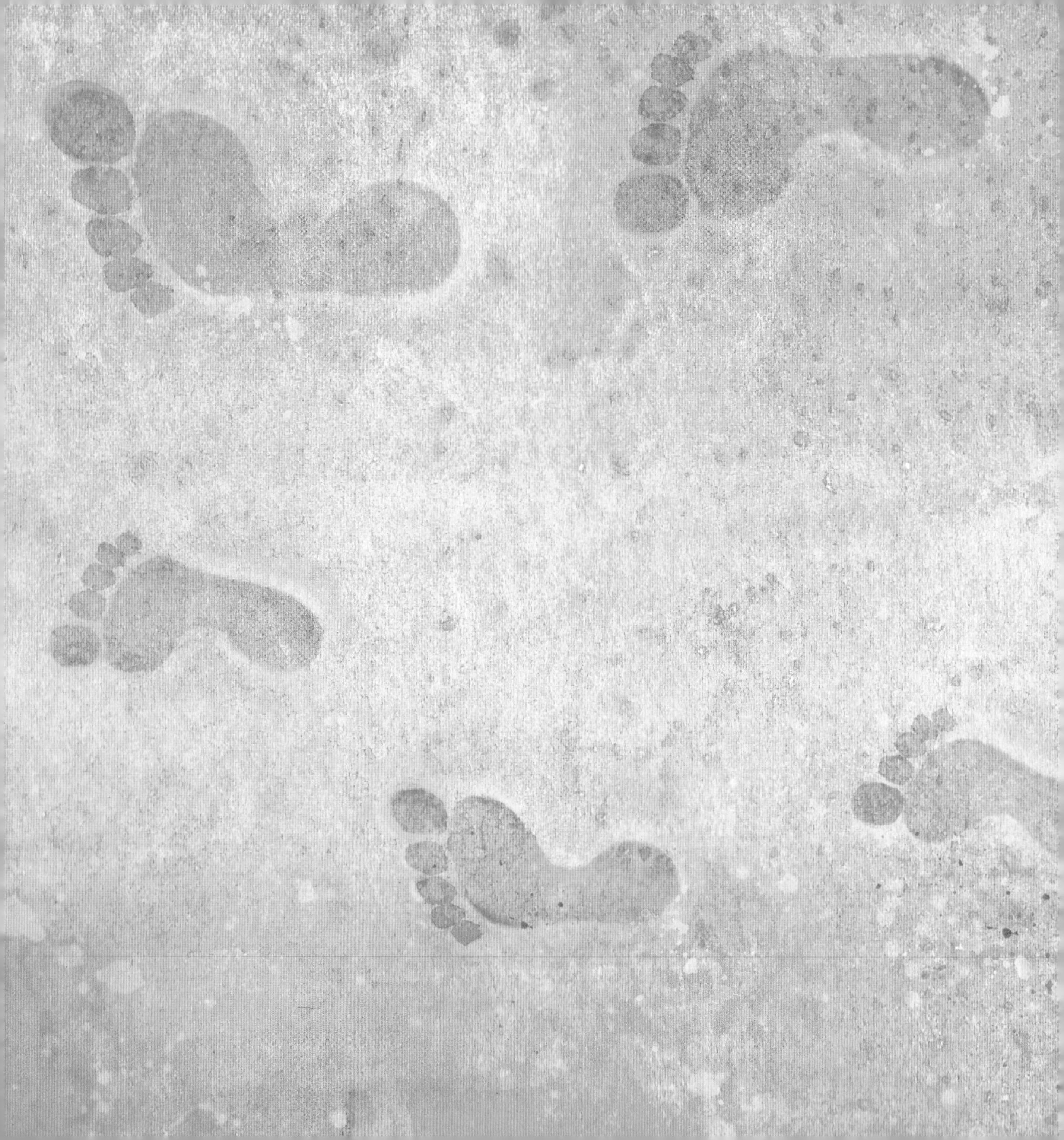